POEMS Just for Me

Festival Poems

Chosen by Brian Moses

Illustrated by Kristina Swarner

WINDMILL BOOKS

Published in 2018 by **Windmill Books**, an Imprint of Rosen Publishing
29 East 21ˢᵗ Street, New York, NY 10010

Editor: Victoria Brooker
Designer: Lisa Peacock

Acknowledgments: The Compiler and Publisher would like to thank the authors for allowing their poems to appear in
this anthology. of poems. Poems © the authors. While every attempt has been made to gain permissions and provide an
up-to-date biography, in some cases this has not been possible and we apologize for any omissions. Should there be any
inadvertent omission, please apply to the Publisher for rectification.

"Eight Candles Burning" was first published in "Them and Us" - Jennifer Curry, Bodley Head,
1993 © Celia Warren 2015

Cataloging-in-Publication Data
Names: Moses, Brian.
Title: Festival poems / compiled by Brian Moses.
Description: New York : Windmill Books, 2018. | Series: Poems just for me | Includes index.
Identifiers: ISBN 9781499483901 (pbk.) | ISBN 9781499483864 (library bound) | ISBN 9781508193135 (6 pack)
Subjects: LCSH: Holidays--Juvenile poetry. | Children's poetry, American. | Children's poetry, English.
Classification: LCC PS3562.E9465 F47 2018 | DDC 811'.54--dc23

Manufactured in China
CPSIA Compliance Information: Batch #BS17WM: For Further Information contact Rosen Publishing, New York, New York at 1-800-237-9932

Contents

Let's Celebrate

Let's celebrate people, such brilliant things
no matter what creed
or color of skin

let's celebrate eyes, every complexion
no matter what shade
we're all perfection

let's celebrate difference, it has a nice ring
no matter what mouth
it giggles and grins

let's celebrate tongues, rich fabulous words
no matter what language
make ourselves heard

let's celebrate home, all kinds of buildings
no matter what place
or country we live in

let's celebrate food, whether spicy or sweet
no matter what meal
we all love to eat

let's celebrate, now, come on dance and sing
because no matter what
you're a great human being!

Sue Hardy-Dawson

The Chinese Dragon

I'm the dragon who dances in the street.
    I'm the dragon in the festival.
I leap and twist on caterpillar feet.
    I'm the dragon who dances in the street.
I snap and snort and stamp to the beat.
    I shiver my scales. I can't keep still.
I'm the dragon who dances in the street.
    I'm the dragon in the festival.

I'm the dragon of red, green, and gold,
    I'm the King of the Chinese New Year.
I come from the land of stories of old.
    I'm the dragon of red and green and gold.
I can breathe out fire or smoke that's cold.
    If you've been good then you've nothing to fear
From the dragon of red and green and gold—
    King of the Chinese New Year.

Catherine Benson

Pancake Day

Pour the pancake mixture
In the frying pan
Swirl it round and round again
And flip it if you can!
WHOOPS!
Pancake on the cooker
Pancake on the door
Pancake on my brother's head
Pancake on the floor!
SO!
Pour the pancake mixture
In the frying pan
Swirl it round and round again
And flip it if you can!
WHOOPS!
Pancake on my daddy
Pancake on his clothes

Pancake on my homework
Pancake on my toes!
SO!
Pour the pancake mixture
In the frying pan
Swirl it round and round again
And flip it if you can!
YUMMMM!
Pancakes on the table
Pancakes on my plate
Pancakes in my tummy
Pancake Day is
GREAT!

Debra Bertulis

Holi, Festival of Color

Throw the waters, colored waters,
Holi Festival's here.

Musicians playing, drummers beating,
Processions leading through the streets.

Joyfully children dance and sing,
Holi the colorful Festival of Spring.

Friends and relations all will meet,
Sweetmeats, balloons, for when they greet.

Throw the waters, colored waters,
For Holi Festival's here!

Punitha Perinparaja

Mother's Day

We really tried to spoil our Mum
On Mother's Day:
Took her breakfast up to bed
On a tray;
Gave her presents, cards, and flowers —
A lovely bunch,
Did the washing up and cleaning,
Cooked the lunch.
Housework? We wouldn't let her
Lift a finger,
Put a CD on of Frank
Her favorite singer.
We made the whole day for our Mum
A real treat,
With lots of lovely things
To drink and eat.
Mum thanked us all and said,
"Today was bliss!
Could you please arrange for every day
To be like this?"

Eric Finney

Children's Day

At school today we're celebrating
Kenji's special day.
(Children's Day in Japan
is every 5th of May.)
Gaily colored carp streamers
hang up in the hall —
a big fish, medium, little,
and a rainbow waterfall.
Kenji's mum looks lovely,
her kimono is so bright.
She showed us how to put it on
and make it look just right.
We've folded paper flowers
and an origami box.
We've seen how Kenji's best shoes
must be worn with special socks!
We're going to taste some rice balls
and crispy crackers, too.
I'd like to do this
every year with Kenji, wouldn't you?

Penny Kent

Eid-ul-Fitr

There's the moon!
I see it!
The sky is bright and clear.
Ramadan is over
for another year.
Mum is cooking special things.
Dad's finding decorations.
Tomorrow there'll be hugs
and gifts from all our close relations.
We'll wear our best clothes
to the mosque
and smile at all our friends.
Eid Mubarak! Eid Mubarak!
The month of fasting ends.

Penny Kent

14

It's Diwali Tonight!

Everything's ready to greet the new year.
Everything's bright with light.
Everyone's dressed up and full of joy.
It's Diwali tonight!

We've lit the lamps to show the way
Up to our front door.
We've sprinkled colored powders
To make pictures on the floor.

We've given each other gifts of sweets
There's lots of delicious food to eat.

Everything's ready to greet the new year.
Everything's bright with light.
Everyone's dressed up and full of joy.
It's Diwali tonight!

John Foster

Harvest Thanks

The brown earth grew the green wheat,
the sunshine turned it gold,
the farmer brought the harvest in
before the year turned cold.
Oh, the farmer brought the harvest in
before the year turned cold.

The fruit trees grew the apples,
the sunshine turned them red,
the farmer brought the fruit in
so we could all be fed.
Oh, the farmer brought the fruit in
so we could all be fed.

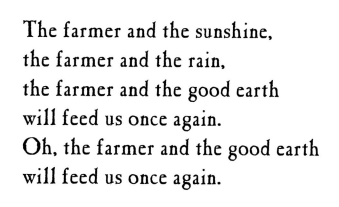

The farmer and the sunshine,
the farmer and the rain,
the farmer and the good earth
will feed us once again.
Oh, the farmer and the good earth
will feed us once again.

So thank you for the raindrops,
and thank you for the sun,
thanks for harvest and for farmers
who grow food for everyone.
Oh, thanks for harvest and for farmers
who grow food for everyone.

Jan Dean

A Hallowe'en Pumpkin

They chose me from my brother: "That's the
Nicest one," they said,
And they carved me out a face and put a
Candle in my head.

And they set me on the doorstep. Oh, the
Night was dark and wild;
But when they lit the candle, then I
Smiled!

Dorothy Aldis

Fireworks!
(a chant for two groups of voices)

Squibs and sparklers
Squibs and sparklers

Golden sprinkles
Golden sprinkles

Shooting stars and Catherine wheels
Shooting stars and Catherine wheels

Fiery flowers
Fiery flowers

Racing rockets
Racing rockets

Whirling windmills
Whirling windmills

Flashing fountains
Flashing fountains

Blazing mountains
Blazing mountains

Light the paper...

Watch them whizzing

Watch them whizzing

Watch them whizzing

BANG!

Judith Nicholls

21

Eight Candles Burning

Three stars are in the sky;
the children have counted them twice.
The menorah is polished,
the matches to hand,
ready to set a candle alight,
today, tomorrow, and every night
until we see
eight candles burning.

Bright as the stars,
the children's eyes and promises.
Parents, grandparents are children again,
thankful for freedom,
happy to set a candle alight,
today, tomorrow, and every night
until we see
eight candles burning.

Around the table
faces are glowing at stories retold.
Like the flame of a match
hearts are burning,
eager to set a candle alight,
today, tomorrow, and every night
until we see
eight candles burning.

Celia Warren

Long, Long Ago

Winds through the olive trees
Softly did blow,
Round little Bethlehem
Long, long ago.

Sheep on the hillside lay
Whiter than snow;
Shepherds were watching them,
Long, long ago.

Then from the happy sky,
Angels bent low,
Singing their songs of joy,
Long, long ago.

For in a manger bed,
Cradled we know,
Christ came to Bethlehem,
Long, long ago.

Anon

Christmas Eve

I'm trying to sleep on Christmas Eve
but I really can't settle down,
and I don't want to lie
with wide open eyes
till the morning comes around.

I hear Mum and Dad downstairs,
doing their best to keep quiet,
and although I'm in bed
with my favorite ted,
in my head there's a terrible riot.

I'm thinking of Christmas morning
and all the presents I'll find,
but what if I've missed
something good off my list,
it keeps going round in my mind.

Mum has been baking all day
making rolls, mince pies, and cake,
and I know quite well
it's this heavenly smell
that's keeping me wide awake.

Now Dad says Father Christmas
won't leave any presents for me.
"Make no mistake,
if you're still awake,
he'll pass you by, you'll see!"

But I've tried and I've tried and I've tried
and I keep rolling round in my bed,
I still can't sleep,
and I'm fed up with sheep
so I'm counting reindeer instead!

Brian Moses

Happy New Year

Tick, tock, tick, tock
Can you hear the ticking
Of the big, big clock?

It is ticking out the hours
It is ticking out the day
It is ticking every moment
As we sleep or play

Tick, tock, tick, tock
Can you hear the ticking
Of the big, big clock?

Tonight is the night
When the clock will chime
And tick for the old year
One last time

Tick, tock, tick, tock
Can you hear the ticking
Of the big, big clock?

Now it's midnight
Give a big, big cheer
For the clock is ticking
For a Happy New Year!

Brenda Williams

Further information

Websites

For web resources related to the subject of this book, go to:
www.windmillbooks.com/weblinks and select this book's title.

About the Poets:

Dorothy Aldis (1896-66) was a children's poet who lived in Chicago. She published 29 books in her lifetime. After she passed away, she was given the title "The Poet Laureate of Young Children."

Catherine Benson spent much of her childhood in Scotland. Her poems have been published in many anthologies for children. She's passionate about nature and has reared many a creature from birds, cats, and mice to geckos, beetles, frogs, and stick insects, though of course, not all at the same time!

Debra Bertulis' life-long passion is the written and spoken word, and she is the author of many published poems for children. She is regularly invited to schools where her workshops inspire pupils to compose and perform their own poetry. Debra lives in Herefordshire, where she enjoys walking the nearby Welsh hills and seeking out second-hand book shops!

Jan Dean likes ice cream and earrings. Her penguin earrings are special favorites. (Also the giraffes.) She likes singing, drawing, and making bread. She visits schools to perform her poems and write new poems with classes. She likes it best when the poems explode all over the whiteboards and dribble down the walls.

Sue Hardy-Dawson has been widely published in children's poetry anthologies and long-listed for the 2014 Manchester Writing for Children Prize. She has an open First Class Honors Degree and has provided workshops, both in schools and for the Foundation for Children and the Arts. As a dyslexic poet, she is especially interested in encouraging reluctant readers and writers.

Eric Finney wrote a number of books for children including *Billy and Me at the Church Hall Sale* and *Billy and Me and the Igloo*. His poems can be found in many

anthologies. He was fond of walking and nearly always returned from his walks with ideas for poems. He lived in Ludlow, England.

John Foster is a children's poet, anthologist, and poetry performer, well-known for his performance as a dancing dinosaur. He has written over 1,500 poems and *The Poetry Chest* containing over 250 of his own poems is published by Oxford University Press. He is a former teacher and the author of many books for classroom use.

Penny Kent: For many years, Penny Kent enjoyed teaching primary school children from thirty-six different countries at International Schools in Tanzania, Turkey, Germany, India, and South Korea. The range of her cultural experiences is reflected in her children's poems, which have been published in many anthologies. She lives in Gloucestershire, England, now, but still travels widely and writes all the time.

Brian Moses lives in Burwash in Sussex where the famous writer Rudyard Kipling once lived. He travels the country performing his poetry and percussion show in schools, libraries and theaters. He has published over 200 books including the series of picture books *Dinosaurs Have Feelings Too*.

Judith Nicholls started in a tiny one-room school in Lincolnshire, England. She has since happily visited over 500 schools to run poetry performances and workshops with children and teachers. She loves gardening, walking, reading, and philosophy discussions with grandchildren! Her first book was *Magic Mirror* and she has since written and compiled around 50 books.

Celia Warren has written over 100 books of children's stories, poems, and puzzles. She grew up in North Lincolnshire, England, raised her children in the West Midlands, and now lives with her husband in South Devon, England. Ideas for poems pop up at the oddest times—from walking in the country to playing table tennis or line-dancing. That's why she always carries a notebook, a pen...and a camera!

Brenda Williams is the internationally published author of seven children's books. A former teacher, she has over one thousand children's poems and action rhymes published and is a reader and performer of poems and stories in schools and at festivals including the Edinburgh International Literacy Festival.

Index of first lines